Table of Contents

This is the story of *Beauty and the Beast*. You can read along with me in your book. You will know it is time to turn the page when you hear the chimes ring like this. . . .
Let's begin now.

Narrator	ROY DOTRICE
Belle	PAIGE O'HARA
Beast	ROBBY BENSON
Gaston	RICHARD WHITE
Maurice	REX EVERHART
LeFou	JESSE CORTI
Lumiere	JERRY ORBACH
Cogsworth	DAVID OGDEN STIERS

Produced by TED KRYCZKO and RANDY THORNTON

Beauty and the Beast

"My father's not crazy! He's a genius!" As Belle spoke, an explosion boomed from her father's cottage, and she took off running.

At the cottage, Belle found her father and told him what the villagers were saying about her. "They think I'm odd, Papa."

"Don't worry, Belle. My invention's going to change everything for us. We won't have to live in this little town forever!"

Belle's father hitched up their horse, Phillipe, and set off for the fair with his new invention. Belle waved. "Good-bye! Good luck!"

But Maurice got lost and accidentally led Phillipe into a bleak, misty forest. As he paused to get his bearings, Maurice saw two yellow eyes staring out of the darkness. It was a wolf! Phillipe reared and bolted away. Terrified, Maurice ran through the forest with the wolves racing behind him. When he reached a tall, heavy gate, Maurice dashed inside, slamming the gate on the wolf, whose sharp teeth snapped at his leg.

Still trembling, Maurice turned to see a huge, forbidding castle. "Hello? I've lost my horse, and I need a place to stay for the night."

"Of course, Monsieur! You are welcome here!" Maurice whirled around. There was no one in sight! Then he looked down and saw a mantel clock with a stern, frowning face. Beside him stood a smiling candelabra! Maurice grabbed the clock and examined it. "This is impossible. Why—you're alive!"

The enchantress had also turned all the Prince's servants into household objects. As Cogsworth, the mantel clock, protested, Lumiere, the candelabra, showed Maurice into the drawing room. There he met a friendly teapot named Mrs. Potts and her son, a cute teacup named Chip. Suddenly, the door flew open. A voice boomed, "There's a stranger here. . . ."

Maurice jumped out of his chair. In the shadows lurked a large, hulking figure. "Please . . . I needed a place to stay!"

"I'll give you a place to stay!" The Beast grabbed Maurice and dragged him out of the room.

Back home at the cottage, Belle heard a knock at the door and opened it. "Gaston! What a 'pleasant' surprise!"

"Belle, there's not a girl in town who wouldn't love to be in your shoes. Do you know why? Because I want to marry you!"

"Gaston, I'm speechless! I'm sorry, but . . . but . . . I just don't deserve you."

As Gaston left, he tripped and fell in the mud. When Belle peeked out, she saw that the villagers had gathered in her yard hoping to see a wedding. The vicar and all Gaston's friends saw him humiliated!

After the villagers and a very angry Gaston left, Belle ran outside to feed the chickens. There she found Phillipe, alone. "Phillipe! What are you doing here? Where's Papa?"

The horse whinnied anxiously. Frightened, Belle leaped onto Phillipe and returned to the mysterious forest. Soon, they found the castle.

"What is this place?" Belle tried to steady Phillipe. Then she saw Maurice's hat on the ground.

Belle hurried inside the gloomy castle and wandered down the vast, deserted corridors.

"Papa? Are you here? It's Belle." No one replied, but Belle didn't know that the enchanted objects had seen her.

With joy, Lumiere danced around the mantel clock. "Don't you see? She's the one! She has come to break the spell!"

Without noticing them, Belle continued to search for her father.

Finally, Belle discovered Maurice locked in a tower. "Papa! We have to get you out of there!" Suddenly she heard a voice from the shadows.

"What are you doing here?"

Belle gasped. "Please let my father go. Take me instead!"

"You would take his place?"

Belle asked the voice to step into the light and was horrified when she saw the huge, ugly Beast. To save her father, however, Belle agreed to stay in the Beast's castle forever.

The Beast dragged Maurice out of the castle and threw him into a carriage that would return him to town. There, the inventor stumbled into a tavern where Gaston was surrounded by his friends. "Please, I need your help! A horrible beast has Belle locked in a dungeon!"

"Did it have cruel, sharp fangs?" one villager sneered.

Maurice grabbed the man's coat. "Yes! Yes! Will you help me out?"

"We'll help you out, old man." Gaston and his pals tossed the inventor out of the tavern. But Maurice's wild story gave Gaston an idea.

At the castle, Belle nervously followed the Beast upstairs. He paused for a moment. "The castle is your home now, so you can go anywhere you like . . . except the West Wing."

Belle stared back. "What's in the West Wing?"

"It's forbidden!" Glaring, the Beast opened the door to her room. "You will join me for dinner. That's not a request!"

After the Beast stomped off, Belle flung herself on the bed. "I'll never escape from this prison—or see my father again!"

That night, Belle refused to dine with the Beast. Instead, she crept downstairs to the kitchen. All the enchanted objects fed and entertained her. Then Cogsworth agreed to take her on a tour.

Belle halted beneath a darkened staircase. "What's up there?"

"Nothing, absolutely nothing of interest at all in the West Wing."

But when Cogsworth wasn't looking, Belle slipped away and raced up the staircase to a long hallway lined with broken mirrors.

Belle cautiously opened the doors at the end of the corridor and entered a dank, filthy room strewn with broken furniture, torn curtains, and gray, gnawed bones. The only living object was a rose, shimmering beneath a glass dome. Entranced, Belle lifted the cover and reached out to touch one soft, pink petal. She did not hear the Beast enter the room.

"I warned you never to come here!" The Beast advanced on Belle. "GET OUT! GET OUT!" Terrified by his rage, she turned and ran.

Belle rushed past Cogsworth and Lumiere as she fled the castle. "Promise or no promise, I can't stay here another minute!"

She found Phillipe, and they galloped through the snow until they met a pack of fierce, hungry wolves. Terrified, the horse reared and Belle fell to the ground. When Belle tried to defend Phillipe, the wolves turned on her, snarling. Suddenly, a large paw pulled the animals off her. It was the Beast!

As Belle struggled to her feet, the wolves turned and attacked the Beast, growling fiercely. With a ferocious howl, the Beast flung off his attackers. As the surprised wolves ran off into the woods, the Beast collapsed, wounded.

Belle knew that this was her chance to escape, but when she looked at the fallen Beast, she could not leave him. "Here, lean against Phillipe. I'll help you back to the castle."

Meanwhile, Gaston and LeFou were plotting to have Maurice put into Monsieur D'Arque's insane asylum unless Belle agreed to marry Gaston.

At the castle, Belle cleaned the Beast's wounds and thanked him for saving her life. Later, she was quite surprised when he showed her a beautiful library. "I can't believe it! I've never seen so many books in all my life!"

The Beast smiled for the first time. "Then it's yours!"

That evening Mrs. Potts and the other objects watched Belle read a story to the Beast. They were filled with hope that the Beast and Belle were falling in love.

Gradually, the mood in the castle began to change. Belle and the Beast read together, dined together, and played together in the snow. They even had a snowball fight! When Belle watched the big, awkward Beast try to feed some birds, she realized that he had a kind, gentle side to him—something that she hadn't seen before. In turn, the Beast began to hope that Belle would begin to care for him. He tidied his room, bathed, and dressed up for the evening. He was overjoyed when Belle taught him how to dance.

That evening, the Beast asked Belle if she was happy.

"Yes. I only wish I could see my father. I miss him so much."

"There is a way." The Beast showed Belle the magic mirror. In it, she saw her father lost in the woods, ill from his search for her. When the Beast saw the unhappy look on Belle's face, he decided to let her go, even if it meant that he would never be human again. Before Belle left, he handed her the magic mirror. "Take it with you, so you'll always have a way to look back and remember me."

Heartbroken, the Beast watched as Belle rode off on Phillipe. When she found her poor father in the forest, Belle brought him home to their cottage so she could nurse him back to health. But almost as soon as they arrived, a tall, thin man knocked on the door. It was Monsieur D'Arque! He had come to take her father to an insane asylum!

"No, I won't let you!" Belle blocked the way.

LeFou had also convinced the villagers that Maurice was crazy because he was raving like a lunatic about some terrible beast.

Gaston put his arm around Belle. "I can clear up this little misunderstanding—if you marry me. Just say yes."

"I'll never marry you! My father's not crazy. I can prove it!"

Belle showed them the Beast in the magic mirror. "He's not vicious. He's really kind and gentle."

Enraged, Gaston shouted, "She's as crazy as the old man! I say we kill the Beast!" The mob of villagers locked Belle and her father in the cellar and stormed the Beast's castle.

As the villagers battled the enchanted objects, Gaston forced the Beast onto the castle roof. He clubbed the Beast, who didn't even try to resist. "Get up! Or are you too 'kind and gentle' to fight back?"

"Stop!"

Chip had helped Belle and Maurice escape from the cellar. When the Beast saw Belle, he grabbed Gaston by the throat. But his love for Belle had made him too human. He let Gaston go and faced Belle. Without warning, Gaston stabbed the Beast in the back! The Beast roared. Gaston stepped back and tumbled off the roof to his death.

Wounded, the Beast gazed at Belle before he collapsed. She ran
to him and held him in her arms. "No! Please! I love you!"

Suddenly, the rain began to shimmer. Slowly the Beast opened his eyes, and in astonishment he watched his paws transform into hands. He held them out to Belle. "Belle, it's me!"

Belle hesitated and looked into his eyes. "It is you!" The Prince drew her close and kissed her. Then they watched happily as Cogsworth, Lumiere, Chip, Mrs. Potts, and all the other servants once again become human. True love had finally broken the spell, and everyone danced for joy.

This is the story of *The Little Mermaid.* You can read along with me in your book. You will know it is time to turn the page when you hear the chimes ring like this. . . .
Let's begin now.

Narrator	ROY DOTRICE
Ariel	JODI BENSON
Flounder	JASON MARIN
Scuttle	BUDDY HACKETT
Sir Grimsby	BEN WRIGHT
Eric	CHRISTOPHER BARNESI
Ursula	PAT CARROLL
Sebastian	SAMUEL E. WRIGHT
Triton	KENNETH MARS
Eels (Flotsam and Jetsam)	PADDI EDWARDS

Produced by TED KRYCZKO and RANDY THORNTON

THE LITTLE MERMAID

Once upon a time, a little mermaid named Ariel frolicked below the ocean, exploring the hulls of sunken ships. She beckoned to her playmate, a roly-poly fish. "Come on, Flounder! I'm sure this old boat has lots of human treasure aboard."

"I'm not g-g-going in there! It's spooky."

"Don't be such a guppy! Follow me!" Swimming inside the ship's cabin, Ariel discovered some rusted silverware. "Oh, my gosh! Have you ever seen anything so wonderful?"

Ariel swam to the water's surface and found her seagull friend.
"Scuttle, do you know what this is?" She held up the fork.
"Judging from my expert knowledge of humans . . . it's obviously
a . . . a . . . dinglehopper! Humans use these to straighten their hair!"

"Thanks, Scuttle! It's perfect for my collection." Ariel dove to an undersea grotto, where she kept her treasures from the human world. She hid her collection there because her father, the sea king, forbade merpeople to have any contact with humans.

That night, Ariel saw strange lights shimmering over the ocean and swam up to investigate.

On the surface, she gaped at fireworks that flared above a large sailing ship.

Scuttle soared down through the flickering colors. "Some celebration, huh, sweetie? It's the birthday of the human they call Prince Eric."

Forgetting her father's decree, Ariel peered at the young man on deck. "I've never seen a human this close. He's very handsome."

Aboard the ship, Eric's adviser, Sir Grimsby, motioned for the crew's attention. "It is now my privilege to present our esteemed prince with a very expensive, very large birthday gift—a marble statue carved in his exact likeness! Of course, I had hoped it would be a wedding present."

The prince glanced away, gazing at the sea. "Don't start, Grim. The right girl's out there . . . somewhere."

Far beneath the ocean, the wicked sea witch, Ursula, used her magic to spy on Ariel. "My, my, the daughter of the great sea king, Triton, in love with a human! A prince, no less. Her daddy will love that! Serves him right, that miserable old tyrant! Banishing me from his palace, just because I was a little ambitious.

"Still, this headstrong, lovesick girl may be the key to my revenge on Triton. She'll be the perfect bait—when I go fishing for her father!"

On the surface, a sudden storm whipped across the ocean. The prince took charge. "Stand fast! Secure the rigging!"

Without warning, a huge bolt of lightning struck the vessel. Sir Grimsby slid across the deck. "Eric, look out! The mast is falling!"

Ariel watched in horror. "Eric's been knocked into the water! I've got to save him!"

With the storm swirling about her, Ariel desperately searched for Eric. "Where is he? If I don't find him soon—wait, there he is!"

Diving beneath the waves, Ariel spotted the unconscious figure. "He's sinking fast! I've got to pull him out of the water . . . before he drowns!" She took hold of Eric and, using all her strength, managed to drag him to the surface.

As the storm died down, Ariel dragged the unconscious prince to shore. "He's still breathing! He must be alive."

A crab scuttled across the sand. It was Sebastian, the sea king's music director. "Ariel, get away from that human! Your father forbids contact with them, remember?"

"But Sebastian, why can't I stay with him? Why can't I be part of his world?" And she sang a haunting melody that voiced her longing to be with Eric forever.

A moment later, Ariel was back in the water, and Sir Grimsby was kneeling beside Eric. "You really delight in these sadistic strains on my blood pressure, don't you?"

"Grim, a girl rescued me. . . . She was singing in the most beautiful voice."

"I think you've swallowed a bit too much seawater! Here, Eric, let me help you to your feet."

Back at the coral palace, Triton noticed Ariel floating about as if in a dream. Summoning Sebastian, the sea king smiled. "You've been keeping something from me. I can tell Ariel's in love."

"I tried to stop her! I told her to stay away from humans!"

"Humans! Ariel is in love with a human?"

Triton found Ariel in her grotto. She was staring at Eric's statue, which Flounder had retrieved after the storm. "How many times have I told you to stay away from those fish-eating barbarians! Humans are dangerous!"

"But, Daddy, I love Eric!"

"So help me, Ariel, I am going to get through to you no matter what it takes!" Raising his trident, the sea king destroyed all her treasures. Then he stormed off, leaving Ariel in tears.

As she wept, two eels slithered up to her. "Don't be scared. We represent someone who can help you!"

Ariel followed them to Ursula's den.

"My dear, sweet child! I haven't seen you since your father banished me from his court! To show that I've reformed, I'll grant you three days as a human to win your prince. Before sunset on the third day, you must get him to kiss you. If you do, he's yours forever. But if you don't, you'll be mine!"

Ariel took a deep breath and nodded. The sea witch smiled deviously. "Oh, yes, I almost forgot. We haven't discussed payment. I'm not asking much. All I want is—your voice!"

Sebastian, who had followed Ariel, scurried out of hiding. "Don't listen, Ariel! She is a demon!"

But Ursula had already used her powers to capture Ariel's beautiful voice in a seashell and transform the little mermaid into a human!

Aided by Sebastian and Flounder, Ariel used her new legs to swim awkwardly to shore. There she found Prince Eric walking his dog.

"Down, Max, down! I'm awfully sorry, miss." Eric studied Ariel as she shied away from the animal. "Hey, wait a minute. Don't I know you? Have . . . have we ever met?"

Ariel opened her mouth to answer, forgetting that her voice was gone. The prince lowered his eyes. "You can't speak—or sing, either? Then I guess we haven't met."

Eric gently took Ariel's arm. "Well, the least I can do is make amends for my dog's bad manners. C'mon, I'll take you to the palace and get you cleaned up."

At the royal estate, Ariel was whisked upstairs by a maid. Grimsby discovered the prince staring glumly out the window. "Eric, be reasonable! Young ladies don't go around rescuing people, then disappearing into thin air!"

"I'm telling you, she was real! If only I could find her . . ."

The following afternoon, Eric took Ariel for a rowboat ride across a lagoon. Sebastian swam below them. "Almost two days gone and that boy hasn't puckered up once! How she gonna get that boy to kiss her? Maybe this will help create the romantic mood."

He began conducting a sea-creature chorus. "C'mon and kiss the girl. . . . The music's working! Eric's leaning over to kiss Ariel." As the prince bent toward her, the boat tipped and both Eric and Ariel fell into the water!

From her ocean lair, Ursula saw them tumble into the lagoon. "That was too close for comfort! I can't let Ariel get away that easily!"

She began concocting a magic potion. "Soon Triton's daughter will be mine! Then I'll make the sea king writhe and wriggle like a worm on a hook!"

The next morning, Scuttle flew into Ariel's room to congratulate her. The prince had announced his wedding!

Overjoyed at the news, Ariel hurried downstairs. She hid when she saw Eric introducing Grimsby to a mysterious dark-haired maiden. The prince seemed hypnotized. "Vanessa saved my life. We're going to be married onboard ship at sunset."

Ariel drew back, confused. She was the one who had rescued Eric! Fighting tears, she fled the palace.

Sebastian found Ariel sitting on the dock, watching the wedding ship leave the harbor.

Suddenly, Scuttle crash-landed beside them. "When I flew over the boat, I saw Vanessa's reflection in a mirror! She's the sea witch in disguise! And she's wearing a seashell containing Ariel's voice. We've got to stop the wedding!"

Sebastian splashed into the water. "Flounder, you help Ariel swim out to that boat! I'm going to get the sea king!"

Dripping wet, Ariel climbed aboard the ship just before sunset as Eric and the maiden were about to be married.

Before Vanessa could say "I do," Scuttle and an army of his friends attacked her. In the scuffle, the maiden's seashell necklace crashed to the deck, freeing Ariel's voice. Suddenly, Vanessa sounded like the sea witch. "Eric, get away from her!"

Ariel smiled at the prince. "Oh, Eric, I wanted to tell you . . ."

Ursula grinned. "You're too late! The sun has set!"

Ariel felt her body changing back into a mermaid. As she dove into the water, the witch transformed her into a helpless sea plant. "You're mine, angelfish! But don't worry, you're merely the bait to catch your father! Why, here he is now!"

"I'll make a deal with you, Ursula, just don't harm my daughter!"

Instantly, Triton was changed into a tiny plant, and Ariel resumed her mermaid form. She stood heartbroken before Ursula, now queen of the ocean.

Suddenly, Prince Eric appeared. He tossed a harpoon at the sea witch, hitting her in the arm. Ursula snatched up the king's trident. "You little fool!"

As the sea witch pointed the weapon at Eric, Ariel rammed into her, knocking the trident loose.

"Eric, we have to get away from here!" The moment they surfaced, huge tentacles shot out of the ocean.

"Eric, we're surrounded. Look out!" Ariel gasped as an enormous monster emerged. It was the sea witch!

Using her new powers, the witch commanded the waters into a deadly whirlpool. Several old sunken ships rose to the surface.

The prince struggled aboard one of the boats. As Ursula loomed above Ariel, Eric plunged the sharp prow through the sea witch, destroying her. The mighty force sent Eric reeling toward shore.

As the unconscious prince lay on the beach, Ariel perched on a rock and gazed at him. Triton and Sebastian watched from afar.

"She really does love him, doesn't she, Sebastian?"

The sea king waved his trident, and Ariel was once again human.

The next day, she and Prince Eric were married onboard the wedding ship. As they kissed, the humans and merpeople sent up a happy cheer, linked at last by the marriage of two people whose love was as deep as the sea and as pure as a young girl's voice.

This is the story of *Snow White and the Seven Dwarfs*.
You can read along in your book. You'll know it's time
to turn the page when you hear this sound. . . .
Let's begin now.

Narrator	MARCY D'ARCY
The Queen	EDA REISS MERIN
The Prince	JERRY WHITMAN
Magic Mirror	TONY JAY
The Huntsman	PETER RENADAY
Snow White	MARY KAY BERGMAN
Doc	HAL SMITH
Grumpy	COREY BURTON

Adapted by RANDY THORNTON
Produced by RANDY THORNTON and TED KRYCZKO

Once upon a time, there lived a lovely little princess named Snow White. Her vain and wicked stepmother, the Queen, feared that one day Snow White's beauty would surpass her own. So she dressed the little princess in rags and forced her to work as a servant in the castle.

Each day, the Queen consulted her Magic Mirror. "Magic Mirror on the wall, who is the fairest one of all?"

As long as the mirror responded in the Queen's favor, Snow White was safe.

One day, as Snow White was drawing water from a well, she made a wish. She wished that the one she loved would find her, and she dreamed about how nice he would be.

As she gazed into the wishing well, she saw another face reflected in the water. It belonged to a handsome prince. "Hello. Did I frighten you? Please don't run away!"

But the startled princess had fled to her balcony, where she could watch him from afar.

At that moment, the Queen was spying on Snow White and the Prince. When she saw them together, she flew into a jealous rage and rushed to her Magic Mirror, demanding an answer.

"Famed is thy beauty, Majesty, but hold! A lovely maid I see. Rags cannot hide her gentle grace. She is more fair than thee."

"Alas for her! Reveal her name."

"Lips red as a rose, hair black as ebony, skin white as snow . . ."

"SNOW WHITE!"

Furious, the Queen sent for her Huntsman. "Take Snow White far into the forest. Find some secluded glade where she can pick wildflowers. And there, my faithful Huntsman, you will kill her!"

"But, Your Majesty, the little princess!"

"Silence! You know the penalty if you fail."

Knowing that he dare not disobey the Queen, the Huntsman led Snow White into the forest. But when it came time for him to harm Snow White, he stopped and fell to his knees. "I can't do it. Forgive me, Your Highness!"

"Why, why—I don't understand."

"The queen is mad! She's jealous of you. She'll stop at nothing. Now quick, child—run, run away. Hide in the woods! Anywhere! And never come back!"

Frightened and alone, Snow White ran into the forest. Blazing eyes peered out at her from the darkness. Eerie shrieks pierced the air. The branches of trees grabbed at her. Finally she could run no farther and collapsed to the ground, sobbing.

When Snow White looked up, she saw several forest animals gathered around her.

"Hello. Do you know where I can stay? Maybe in the woods somewhere?"

Snow White followed the animals to a charming little cottage in the woods. She knocked on the door, but no one answered. So she went inside.

"Oh, it's adorable! Just like a doll's house. What a cute little chair. Why, there's seven little chairs! There must be seven little children. And by the looks of this table, seven untidy children. I know, I'll clean house and surprise them; then maybe they'll let me stay."

With the help of her animal friends, Snow White cleaned the cottage in no time. Then she decided to check upstairs. "What adorable little beds! And look—they have names carved on them. Doc, Happy, Sneezy, Dopey . . . what funny names for children! And there's Grumpy, Bashful, and Sleepy. I'm a little sleepy myself." Snow White laid down across three of the tiny beds and fell asleep.

Just then, the owners of the cottage came marching home. They weren't children at all, but Seven Dwarfs who worked all day in their diamond mine.

As they came into the clearing, the one named Doc made everyone halt. He peered through his glasses. "Look—our house! The lit's light! The light's lit! Door's open. Chimney's smokin'. Somethin's in there!"

The Dwarfs peeked inside the cottage. Doc gasped. "Why, the whole place is clean!"

Grumpy, true to his name, crossed his arms and glared. "Mark my words, there's trouble a-brewin'. I felt it comin' on all day."

Suddenly, the Dwarfs thought they heard a sound. Doc looked towards the stairs. "I-it-it's up there. In the bedroom."

Cautiously, the seven little men went to investigate. Doc slowly opened the door and peered in. "Why, i-it-it's a girl."

As the Dwarfs approached the sleeping princess, she began to stir. "She's wakin' up! Hide!"

Doc dashed behind the beds, and the other Dwarfs ran after him.

Snow White yawned and stretched. Then she noticed seven pairs of eyes looking at her over the end of beds. She sat up, smiling. "How do you do?"

"How do you do what?" Grumpy folded his arms, scowling.

Snow White laughed. "Let me guess. You must be Grumpy."

"Heh! I know who I am. Who are you?"

"Oh, how silly of me. I'm Snow White."

"The princess?" Doc looked very impressed.

But Grumpy frowned. "Tell her to go back where she belongs."

Snow White pleaded with her hosts. "Please don't send me away! If you do, the Queen will kill me!"

Grumpy shook his head. "The Queen's an old witch. If she finds you here, she'll swoop down and wreak her vengeance on all of us!"

"Oh, she'll never find me here. And if you let me stay, I'll keep house for you. I'll wash and sew and sweep and cook. . . ."

"Cook!" Doc rubbed his tummy. "Hooray! She stays!"

Back in the castle, the wicked Queen stood before her mirror. "Magic Mirror on the wall, who now is the fairest one of all?"

"Beyond the seventh fall, in the cottage of the Seven Dwarfs, Snow White still lives, fairest one of all."

"I've been tricked! I'll go myself to the Dwarfs' cottage in the woods. I'll go in a disguise so complete, no one will suspect me."

The Queen concocted a magic potion, then transformed herself into an ugly old peddler woman. "And now, a special sort of death for one so fair. What should it be? Ah, a poisoned apple! One taste, and Snow White's eyes will close forever, only to be revived by Love's First Kiss. No fear of that! The Dwarfs will think she's dead!"

Back at the cottage, Snow White was saying good-bye to the Dwarfs as they set off for work. As she kissed each one on the head, Doc stood close by. "Now don't forget, my dear, the old Queen's a sly one. Full of witchcraft, so beware."

Then Grumpy frowned. "Now, I'm warnin' ya, don't let nobody or nothin' in the house."

Snow White smiled at him. "Why, Grumpy, you do care!"

"Heh!"

Shortly after the Dwarfs left, the old peddler woman appeared at the cottage. "All alone, my pet?" Snow White nodded as the old woman sniffed the air. "Makin' pies?"

"Yes, gooseberry pies."

"Ahh, it's apple pies that make the menfolks' mouths water. Pies made with apples like these." She lifted a shiny red apple from her basket. "Like to try one, dearie, hmm? Go on, have a bite."

Sensing that Snow White was in danger, several birds swooped down on the woman, knocking the apple out of her hand. Snow White tried to shoo the birds away. "Stop it! Go away! Shame on you, frightening the poor old lady."

"Oh, my heart! Oh, my. My poor heart. Take me into the house and let me rest. A drink of water, please."

Unable to make Snow White understand, the birds and animals raced to alert the Dwarfs. At the mine, they pulled and tugged at the confused little men. Grumpy growled. "What ails these crazy critters? They ain't actin' this way for nothin'."

Doc thought about it. "Maybe it's—the Queen!"

Grumpy galloped off on the back of a deer. "Snow White's in danger! We've gotta save her!"

Meanwhile, the Queen picked up the poisoned apple. "Because you've been so good to poor old Granny, I'll share a secret with you. This is no ordinary apple. It's a magic wishing apple!"

"A wishing apple? Really?"

"Yes. One bite and all your dreams will come true."

The old woman grinned at the princess. "Perhaps there's someone you love?"

Snow White remembered her prince. "Well, there is someone."

"I thought so. Old Granny knows a young girl's heart. Now make a wish and take a bite."

Snow White did so. "Oh, I feel strange."

A moment later, she fell to the ground.

A sudden storm began to rage as the Dwarfs reached the
cottage, where they found the lifeless Snow White. Through the
rain, Grumpy spotted the old hag disappearing into the forest.
"There she goes, men. After her!"

The Dwarfs chased the Queen up a steep cliff. "You little
fools. I'll crush yer bones!"

She tried desperately to pry a boulder loose to crush them.
Suddenly, a bolt of lightning shattered the ledge, sending
the wicked Queen into the valley below.

Though the evil Queen was gone forever, the princess was still locked in her spell. So beautiful was she, even in death, the Dwarfs could not find it in their hearts to bury her.

Doc brushed away a tear. "Let's make her a coffin out of glass and gold. That way, we can still see her and keep constant watch by her side."

The Prince heard of the beautiful maiden who slept in the glass coffin. He rode to the cottage of the Seven Dwarfs, and they took him to Snow White. Gently, he kissed her. Then, slowly, her eyes began to open. The spell was broken. Love's First Kiss had brought her back to life!

Snow White's wish finally came true. She bid the Seven Dwarfs
good-bye as the handsome prince swept her into his arms.
Soon wedding bells rang, echoing throughout the forest.
From then on, Snow White and her Prince Charming lived in
their castle in the clouds . . . happily ever after.

nce upon a tim

cold night, an old beg

return for shelter fro

her away. Suddenly sh

To punish the Prin

she gave him a magic

would bloom until his

love another and earn

petal fell.

...woman named Belle

...ople and then rushed

...r gave her a book as

...favorite! Far-off

...ce in disguise . . . Oh,

As Belle walked, a handsome hunter named Gaston ran after her. "Belle, the whole town's talking about you. It's not right for a woman to read! It's about time you got your nose out of those books and paid attention to more important things—like me."

Belle tried to get away without being rude, but Gaston's friend LeFou joined them and began to insult her father, an inventor.